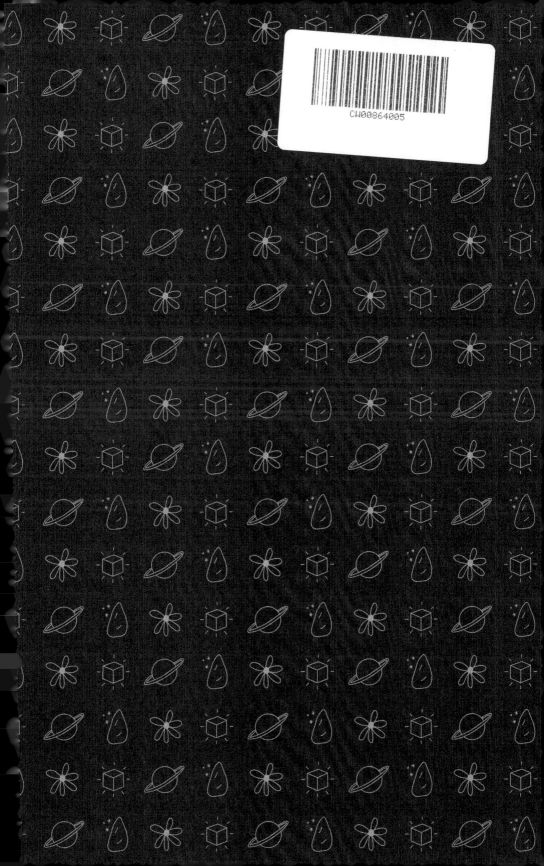

Copyright ©BubblesBooks, 2021
Author: Pol L. Grau
Illustration: Silvia Roma
Design and Layout: Silvia Roma
Translation and editing: Catherine Stephenson

Editorial Bubblebooks
www.bubblesbooks.com

STORIES TO TURN THE WORLD UPSIDE DOWN.

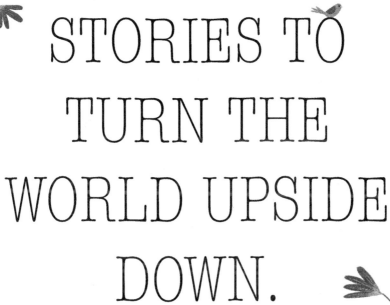

WELCOME!

FOUR STORIES AWAIT YOU, ADVENTURES
INSPIRED BY THE VALUES OF CURIOSITY, HONESTY,
ENVIRONMENTAL SUSTAINABILITY AND INDIVIDUAL
DIFFERENCES. A GROUP OF CHILDREN WILL TAKE YOU WITH
THEM TO FAR-AWAY PLANETS, TO TAME WILD ANIMALS, INTERRUPT
IMPORTANT ADULT MEETINGS AND FIGHT INJUSTICE. ALL THIS IN
JUST ONE BOOK? AMAZING!
IF YOU THINK ABOUT IT, READING A BOOK IS LIKE WATCHING A VIDEO
ONLINE, BUT IN YOUR MIND, WHICH IS EVEN BETTER. PLUS, THE GOOD
THING IS THAT, HOWEVER LONG YOU DO IT FOR, NOBODY WILL TELL YOU
OFF. NOT CONVINCED YET?
LET'S HAVE A GO.
LISTEN CAREFULLY: YOU'RE IN THE COUNTRYSIDE. IT'S A SUNNY
DAY. THERE'S A RED FARMHOUSE AND A WINDMILL. OK. THERE'S
ALSO AN OSTRICH. AN OSTRICH WITH BINOCULARS, LOOKING
AROUND. WHAT'S HE LOOKING AT? AT YOU? AARGH! YOU
STARTLED HIM! DID YOU SEE? HE RAN AWAY AS FAST
AS HE COULD!
NOW YOU'RE READY TO TURN THE
WORLD UPSIDE DOWN.

THE SMALL
INTERGALACTIC TRIBE
FROM OUTER SPACE

A tale to turn an entire planet upside down

The story takes place somewhere far, far away from where you live, of that I'm certain! Not in a nearby street, nor the next town. No, no, much, much further! So, so far away, that it's not even in our galaxy – imagine! There, deep in the dark depths of the universe, a small asteroid was flying through outer space.

It wasn't just any asteroid, because it was also home to a group of children. Yes, yes that's right, home to a group of children. They called themselves "The Small Intergalactic Tribe from Outer Space". What a name!

RUFI was the eldest. She always wore a crown of coloured feathers and was, undoubtedly, the wisest and most patient.
She'd say, "Let's share the sweets of peace."

Then there was **BON-BON**, who specialised in making bad jokes and wore stylish sunglasses.

"My name is Bon, Bon-Bon," is how she'd introduce herself.

And **RAMAN**, a mathematical genius who always carried a notebook and some colouring pencils with him.

"Maths is the language of nature," he'd say.

And last but not least, **NIL**, the baby ninja! The fastest baby in the universe!

"ZZZZ ZZZZ."

He was sleeping, of course.

They were a family, and were always up for their next adventure. Their asteroid was fired by LifeSparks, the energy of life itself. What kind of fuel is that? Well, you could explain it as the curiosity to discover new things. So, the more the children of the tribe learned, the further they could go! Easy. If they wanted to continue traveling through the infinite cosmos, all they had to do was make a few stops here and there to explore new places.

They'd bring back a souvenir from each journey and each space night they'd sit around a campfire and relive their best adventures.

"Tell us the story about Planet Far West!" said Raman.

"No, we've heard that one too many times. The one about Planet Prehistoric and the Monstrosaurus tooth!" Bon-Bon replied.

"Zzzzz" snored Nil.

"Shush everyone," said Rufi. "I know which one - the most epic and amazing adventure we've ever had!"

"The one about?" asked Raman.
"Yes, that one," replied the chief.
         Rufi stood up and started looking in the
chest for the souvenir they'd brought back from the
epic adventure, when suddenly she landed on her
backside. The asteroid had ground to a halt! And now
it was barely moving – what had happened?
"Raman, damage report please," Rufi requested.
"We're out of fuel," said the mathematician whizz-kid,
his notebook full of calculations.
Bon-Bon cried, "The asteroid is running on reserve!"
         "It'll be ok," Rufi said reassuringly.
         With so many adventures, it had been
         a long time since they'd refuelled with
         LifeSparks. They needed to land on a planet
         very soon so they could learn new things.

Raman unfolded the Great Secret Map of the Universe and did a few sums to pinpoint their current location.

"According to my calculations, we are in the Unknown, Forbidden and Mysterious Nebula!"

How unlucky! The Unknown, Forbidden and Mysterious Nebula was an unexplored and dangerous place. But there was no time to waste! They had to find a planet to land on or they'd be stuck drifting in the nothingness for ever and ever.

Rufi reached for his old telescope. He could make out a grey planet, not that big but not too far away either.

"Hum, I've seen better..." Bon-Bon wasn't sure.

"What shall we do, Rufi?" Raman asked.

"Well, since we don't know if we're going to find anything else any time soon, let's go for it yes! Let's go! Who's with me?"

They all raised their hands to show their support, except for the baby ninja who had just fallen asleep.

"Three against one, the tribe has spoken. We're going on an adventure to the grey planet! Who's piloting?"

"Me, me, me!" cried Bon-Bon and Raman.

Seeing as they couldn't agree, Rufi took the command chair to fly the asteroid, which in fact was much simpler than it might appear. You only had to sit in the chair and tell it where you wanted to go. It was as if the rock were alive and could hear them. No sooner said than done! The asteroid changed course and headed for the grey planet, only able to go at a snail's pace.

"Could this be the planet of the Impossible Equation?" Raman wondered.

"No, no, I think it's Planet Dummyland Five!" Bon-Bon thought aloud.

"Will there be any intelligent life?" Rufi wondered.

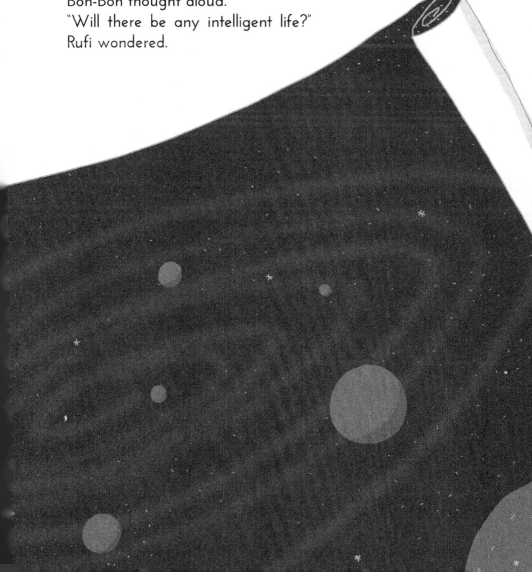

As they drew closer, they got more and more nervous. What would they find this time? It was an unknown, forbidden and mysterious area on the map, and entering was risky!

"There's a city in sight!" Rufi announced.

"You'll see, they're going be zombies." Bon-Bon asserted.

"Nah, I'm sure they'll be very intelligent and we'll learn lots," Raman replied enthusiastically.

"POP-POP-POP" Making a noise like popping soap bubbles, the asteroid finally managed to touch down on the unexplored land. The Small Intergalactic Tribe from Outer Space took a small step, which for them was a giant leap.

Their mission was clear: to observe everything with curiosity and learn as much as possible. When it was completed, they would tell everything they discovered to the asteroid to fill it up with LifeSparks.

Although the mission was clear, Rufi didn't forget to remind them about the Superimportantrule.

"We absolutely mustn't interfere with the customs of this place. It's vitally important we leave the planet exactly as we found it, understood?"

"Yes!" they answered in unison.

"And I don't want any trouble, like we had on Planet Mattress."

"It was Bon-Bon who started jumping."

"No it wasn't, it was Baby ninja!"

"Zzzzz..."

"See!"

After a very short quarrel, they started off on foot, and in an instant they had arrived in the city.

They had expected all sorts of dangers but their first impression of the planet was a rather sad one. On other adventures, they had seen some beautiful houses, like the huts made of palm leaves on Planet Tropical and the cookie houses on Planet Gretel but these buildings didn't look edible. They were tall - three pine trees high or so - made of concrete, and had tiny, tiny, windows.
"We saw nicer houses on Planet Worms."
"It's mathematically impossible to live in them."

"ATTENTION!" Rufi alerted them. "OUR FIRST CONTACT!"

An alien from the planet was approaching them at a fairly rapid pace. He didn't have any tentacles, or antennae, or anything special. He was just a balding man wearing a dark suit, but he was carrying something that caught their interest.

"What is that?"
"A piece of glass?"
"A mirror?"

The alien didn't take his eyes off the small screen in his hand. In fact, he was concentrating so hard that he didn't even notice the children and walked straight past them. They breathed a sigh of relief – they wanted to go unnoticed and did not want to bother anyone. A little while later, they saw another alien on the other side of the street. Just like the first, he couldn't take his eyes off his device. Then another went by, and then another, and another, and another, each of them holding a small screen in their hands!

"Told you, they're all zombies," said Bon-Bon. This confirmed her theory.

"There are a lot of people but it feels like everyone is lonely", Rufi reflected.

"They're all going at exactly the same speed," Raman said, looking at his calculations notebook. "That way they'll never meet up!"

Although it was by far the dullest adventure they'd ever had, they decided to tail one of the aliens to see what he was doing.

The alien carried on walking, gazing intently at the small screen. He went into a grey building, sat on a chair and continued looking at the small screen. Then he stood up and walked back out onto the street, without taking his eyes off the small screen. Finally, he walked into another building and lay down on a couch and – you guessed it – kept his eyes pinned on the small screen!

"Booooring" Bon-Bon was starting to get tired of more and more of the same. "I want to study something interesting, like the time we went to Planet Flatulent".

"Oh yes! We learnt about the origin of farts," Raman recalled.

"That was definitely an explosive adventure!"

They laughed when just then, the napping baby ninja did some gassy sound effects to echo that mythical journey.

"Alright everyone! I'm sure there are very curious things out there, let's keep investigating."

Rufi wasn't giving up yet and so they all followed her. Not far from there, on a corner, there was a building that was different from the rest and they moved closer to get a better view. It had a big window and inside there were people sitting at small tables and eating. A restaurant!

The children pressed their faces against the window to get a better look at what they were eating. It was a greenish paste served in a plastic tray, which was inside a cardboard box.

"Do you remember Planet School Canteen?" said Bon-Bon.

"Dear me! Yes, what a stomach ache!" replied Raman.

"Well, I think the food there was better."

What was even more shocking was the fact that not once did the aliens stop looking at their shiny devices. **NOT EVEN WHEN THEY WERE EATING!** Their food could be green, blue or multi-coloured, they wouldn't even notice - they ate it without looking up!

"I'm not sure we're going to get many LifeSparks with these dull people," said BonBon. You could see the disappointment in her face.

"You might be right." Raman did a few quick calculations to confirm his theory.

"Hang on, there's one thing we haven't seen yet - children!" Rufi hadn't lost hope yet.

"It's true! They're always the most fun and interesting thing in each world we visit."

"Except for Planet Cannibal," Bon-Bon pointed out.

"True. That was no fun at all," Rufi replied, shaking her head.

        So they walked up and down but all they found was more of the same – grey buildings and extra-terrestrial people who wouldn't stop looking at the small gadgets, not even to go to the loo! They'd occasionally spot a restaurant h e r e or there, but no signs of children. They'd almost given up when suddenly they heard a bell

and ran over to see what it was.

A school! And there wasn't just one child; there were dozens.

"I told you! Now, pay attention, I'm sure they'll surprise us!"

So they stood there, quietly observing the behaviour of the young extra-terrestrials.

"Hang on a minute. Silence? In the playground? That doesn't make sense."

"Isn't playtime supposed to be louder than Planet Speaker?"

"Zzzz" the baby ninja seemed to like this peace and quiet.

"Let's keep investigating."

But those mini aliens were even duller than the adults. They each stood by themselves, dazed and hypnotised by the shiny device.

EVEN AT PLAYTIME!

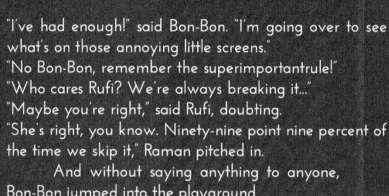

"I've had enough!" said Bon-Bon. "I'm going over to see what's on those annoying little screens."

"No Bon-Bon, remember the superimportantrule!"

"Who cares Rufi? We're always breaking it..."

"Maybe you're right," said Rufi, doubting.

"She's right, you know. Ninety-nine point nine percent of the time we skip it," Raman pitched in.

And without saying anything to anyone, Bon-Bon jumped into the playground and the others followed. They tiptoed over to an alien girl who was by

herself staring at her screen.

"Hello, we come in peace," Rufi greeted the girl.

But nothing happened. The alien was concentrating so hard on moving her finger on the glass of the device, she didn't notice.

"Hello, is anyone there?" Rufi insisted.

"Forget it, she's not answering. We'll have to take action."

In the end, Bon-Bon snatched the gadget out of the girl's hands and the tribe gathered around to finally find out what was on it.

"Let me see, let me see!" Bon-Bon agitated.

"Wow!" said Raman, surprised.

"I don't know what all the fuss was about," said Rufi, disappointed.

The tribe were so focused on the bright glass that they didn't realize that the extra-terrestrial girl was approaching them. She was pointing at them but it didn't really seem like she wanted to hurt them. She started sliding her finger across Rufi's forehead.

"Is she attacking you, chief?" said Raman, alarmed.

"No, she thinks I'm a screen."

And little by little, the other extra-terrestrial children drew close to them. The aliens started to play with what they thought were new screens with legs, that had suddenly appeared in their playground.

"Are we interfering with their customs?"

"I'm not sure to be honest."

"Agu-gu gaga!" The baby ninja was woken up by all the commotion, and was now in a very bad mood indeed.

"Nil's right. At the count of three, let's race to the asteroid. Agreed?"

"But we haven't learnt anything!"

"Of course we have! A curiosity, however dull, is still a curiosity!"

And on "three" they were off like a shot. They didn't want to create havoc on another planet. But before they left, and without anyone noticing, the baby ninja had taken Raman's notebook and colouring pencils and threw them into the middle of the playground. It was his way of getting revenge for having been woken up from his nap.

The Small Intergalactic Tribe from Outer Space returned hurriedly to the asteroid. The first to sit in the command chair was Bon-Bon.

"I've learnt that on Planet Screen you can swap someone's dinner for a plate of flies and they wouldn't even notice. They could be eating invisible toast for breakfast and not realise! Raman, it's your turn. What did you learn?"

"I've learnt that on Planet Screen, if I left a drawing pin on the ground, no one would ever step on it, not in a million years. They always take the same route and at the same speed! Your turn Rufi."

"I've learnt that on Planet Screen, young people hide in an imaginary bubble and play the silence game. And everyone always wins! It's your turn Nil."

"Zzzzz" baby ninja was napping.

And after hearing all those curiosities, the asteroid took off at lightning speed in search of new adventures.

"Is it okay if we name it Planet Screen?" Rufi suggested.

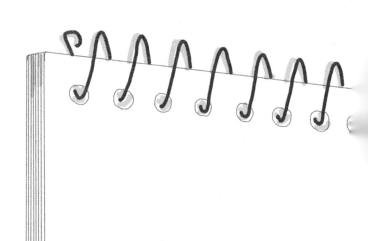

"Seems like a very fitting name," Rafam agreed.

"Planet Screen? Planet Boring more like!" Bon-Bon complained as they left the planet behind.

"I know, we didn't even take away a souvenir," Raman regretted.

"Don't be so sure," Rufi said.

And to everyone's surprise, she pulled one of the gadgets out of her pocket.

"Did you take it?" Raman was worried.

"No, no, the baby ninja had it, I promise."

So they took a step closer and began studying it in depth.

"Is it waterproof?"

"Does it bend?"

"Does it melt?

"Let's see what's inside!"

Amid the flood of questions, the whole tribe began to play around with the device, as they edged away from the grey planet. At a distance, it looked peaceful, but maybe up close it was less so.

Meanwhile, the "gift" that Baby Ninja had left the aliens was about to change everything.

In the playground, the alien who had lost her mobile device picked up the notebook and pencils by mistake. She swiped the red pencil across the paper and was surprised to see what had happened. Then she swiped the paper with more colours: red, pink, and turquoise. Drawing those lines woke up something inside her. She soon discovered that she could even draw on the floor. She tossed the notepad into the air and began to draw flowers on the floor. The notebook happened to fall into the hands of a boy, who accidentally dropped the device he was carrying. Confused, he took the notebook and began to play around with it. He tore out one

of the pages and folded it to make a funny prince's crown. He tossed the notebook away and pretended he was riding an imaginary horse.

Like a domino effect, the extra-terrestrial children all left aside their small screens and started looking at each other. It was only a notebook and pencils, but they found a thousand and one different ways to use them: making boats, masks, hairstyles, drawings, poems, and cutout puppets and colouring everything. This was how the planet broke its silence for the first time, making way for laughter, joy and, above all, to look at the world with curiosity.

THE WISHING
ROCK

A tale to turn lies upside down

W hat would it be like to live in a haunted house? A huge, very old one. Encircled by a garden of creepy trees and squeaking swings. With a ghost pirate lurking in the attic and a green alien living in the garage. It would be scary, wouldn't it? Well that's where seven-year old Max lives.

Max has always liked playing by himself. Over time, that has meant he has developed an extraordinary imagination. If you gave him a plastic cup and a string, he'd live out a thousand adventures. He didn't need anything else! That's why when he moved into this house, he was over the moon.

As you can imagine, normally when people talk about haunted things, there's a sensible explanation for it. For starters, Max didn't live alone. There was also his mother, his brother Ian, and the cat, Marrameu. But to tell you the truth, his mother worked a lot so there were some afternoons when the brothers were home alone with the cat. That's why Ian, who was seven years older, always looked after them until she got back from the office.

And that's where the sensible explanation for this haunted house begins. As Ian got bored babysitting, he started telling Max lots of things that would astonish him.

At first, they were just jokes to pass the time:

"A hundred years ago the house belonged to a pirate who kept his treasure in the attic. That's why we're not allowed to go up there."

"Pirate? Wow!"

Then he started exaggerating to appear cleverer:

"I once did a hundred full circles on the garden swing."

"A hundred? Wow!

And when he didn't know what to say, he thought up stories:

"Mum is late because she's a secret government agent and she's protecting us from the alien invasion."

"Aliens? Wow!"

And eventually, he told stories to tease his brother and laugh at him:

"If you feed Marrameu that much, he's going to get fatter, and fatter and he'll turn into a panther!"

"A panther? Wow!"

Since his brother never actually told him that all his tales were fibs and just for fun, Max grew up thinking that his home was a place full of mysteries. As you can imagine, the house felt a bit scary to him. It was only haunted in his imagination but Max had a lot of that.

Since his brother was seven years older, of course they each went about their own ways. So every time Max wandered around the house by himself, and heard a little noise, he could only come up with wildly unbelievable explanations: Ghosts? Aliens? Lions? As a result, Max got scared an awful **LOT**.

But of all the stories Ian had told him, there was one that particularly fascinated Max. In fact, it was the first story he'd told him, right at the beginning when they moved into the big house, when Max was still six and the garden was uncharted territory.

"You see, there, between those two bushes," Ian pointed.

"Yes," Max said, squinting his eyes to get a better look.

"Looks like a normal rock, doesn't it? Well, that's the wishing rock."

"The wishing rock? And... how does it work?"

"It's really easy."

He walked up to the bushes and took three big steps away from them.

"First you take three giant steps away from the bushes"

Then he knelt down, picked up three pebbles from the ground and showed them to him.

"See, you only have three tries. You have to throw the pebble so as it touches the tip of the rock."

Then Ian tapped his forehead with his finger.

"But first think of a wish. Think carefully, because you can only make one per day."

He looked both ways and spotted their mother

in the distance coming towards them carrying a snack. "And when you know what you want," he took a deep breath and said, "I wish I had a snack now!"

He aimed and threw the stone so flew past the two bushes until it just touched the tip of the rock. "Yes! First time." He raised his fist.

Right then, their mother appeared with some sandwiches and juice. Max stood there wide-eyed with amazement.
"Come and have a snack boys," she said.

His wish had just come true! Right under their nose! From that day, Max wholeheartedly trusted Ian. In fact, he was so impressed that every morning he'd try to make a wish. The problem was that, so far, he hadn't managed to hit the rock on any of the three tries.

It must be said, that at first, the "lies" Ian came up with were amusing. He invented them with affection, to amuse his little brother and entertain him. But the more their mother was absent in the afternoons, the more malicious Ian's lies became. In the end, Max believed the house was haunted.

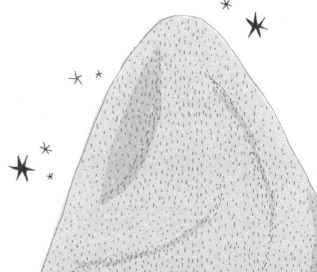

But one of the lies changed everything. One afternoon, not too long ago, Max wanted to play with the video game console but Ian wanted it all to himself and didn't want to share.

"Can I?" Max asked politely.

"Hmm, well okay but with the other controller," Ian agreed reluctantly.

"Thanks!" Max grabbed the second controller and pressed all the buttons.

"See, you're really good!" said Ian.

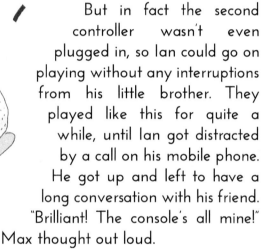

But in fact the second controller wasn't even plugged in, so Ian could go on playing without any interruptions from his little brother. They played like this for quite a while, until Ian got distracted by a call on his mobile phone. He got up and left to have a long conversation with his friend.

"Brilliant! The console's all mine!" Max thought out loud.

It was the first time in ages that he was able to play alone. "How exciting! How exciting! What game can I play?" he wondered. He walked over to the console to change the cartridge and noticed that the second controller wasn't even plugged in. This left him bewildered and uncertain. He'd only ever played with the second controller. What if it had always been unplugged? What if he really wasn't as good as Ian said? What if he had never really played with the console?

When Max realised this, he was angry. No one likes to be duped! But then he remembered all the unbelievable tales Ian had told him and, for the first time, he realised that something didn't add up. Not only that, but his brother was a total fraud. Max had believed for so long that his mother might be hiding an alien in the garage! And what about poor Marrameu? He always took his plate away from him halfway through his meal because he was terrified that he would turn into a beast. Ian had gone too far! Now, Max could have confronted him directly, however, he wanted to teach him a lesson.

"And what if all his lies were to come true?" he murmured to himself. "Surely he'd be the first to be terrified and flee!" And that gave him an idea. He went into the garden and grabbed three pebbles from the ground. Then he walked up to the bushes and took three giant steps away from them. He touched his forehead and wished as hard as he could.

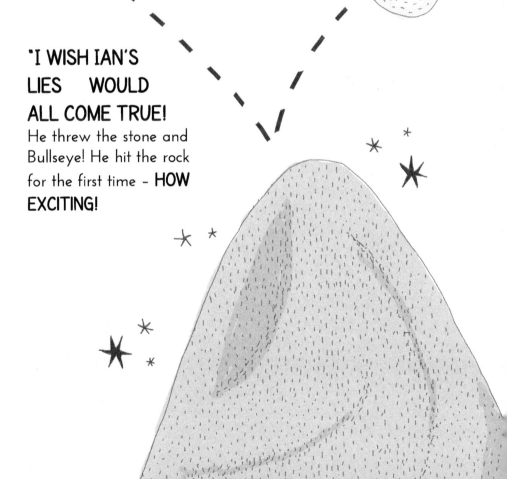

"I WISH IAN'S LIES WOULD ALL COME TRUE!

He threw the stone and Bullseye! He hit the rock for the first time - **HOW EXCITING!**

But, what would happen next? He ran to the kitchen to check. There was Marrameu licking the last bits of food from his bowl. Max rushed over to refill it and encouraged the cat to gobble it all up.

"Come on, little one, turn into a panther, or a tiger."

But that didn't happen. The cat simply gobbled up the extra portion and rolled over to be stroked. Max was deep in thought as he stroked him. If the lies were now true and that didn't work, did that mean it was actually true? Or not? How confusing! If he'd known he was going to hit the rock, he could have wished for something practical, like a dessert.

Then suddenly it dawned on him and he understood – even the wishing rock was a lie! What a fool he'd been! He'd always believed it was real. Now he felt a bit sad and silly for believing the lies, but he also suddenly grew up a little. Now calmer, he mustered up the courage to go into the games room and talk to his brother. The time had come to find out the whole truth.

He opened the door and there was Ian glued to the game console. Max sat next to him, ready to have an honest conversation, but his older brother only had eyes for the screen. He would have to take a different approach.

"Can I?" asked Max.
"Okay sure, but use the second controller."
　　　　Max sighed and picked up the other controller. He was ready to say what he thought, but when he pressed the buttons he noticed something strange – he was actually playing! And he was actually doing well! A jump here, a fireball there, and...
"I've won, I've won!" Max jumped for joy.
"But how, how is that even possible?! Ian stammered.
　　　　He rushed over to check if the controller was still unplugged and, indeed, it was. Ian looked shaken, and Max had a cheeky grin on his face.
"So, a rematch then?" he challenged him.
"No, no. Oh look, it's late!" And just then the doorbell rang.
"That's the door" Ian exclaimed. "I'll going to go and see who it is, stay here."

Max quietly followed Ian as his brother ran off to see who it was. Since they weren't allowed to open the door to strangers, Ian peeped through the spyhole. He saw a man and a woman wearing smart black suits and shades, and the woman was holding a box.

"Who are you?" Ian asked prudently.

"Our identity is secret and confidential," they replied from the other side of the closed door.

"We're not allowed to open the door to sales people, so go away," the boy replied.

"We're not sales people, we're government agents."

"But shhhh! It's a secret!" the other one added.

"What do you want?"

"We have a top secret parcel for your mother."

"She's not here and I'm not sure when she'll be back," Ian answered, getting annoyed.

"Then we'll leave it here. Make sure she gets it. It is vitally important for the safety of the planet. You'll do that won't you?

"Yes, yes, I promise."

The agents left the box outside the front door. After they left, Ian opened the door and brought the box inside. It was quite a large box, but very light. What could it be? The curiosity was eating away at him. He hurried to the kitchen to open it and Max quickly followed.

"Were they secret agents? What's that box?" asked Max.

Completely ignoring him, Ian picked up a pair of scissors to cut the thick tape around the box, but he hadn't come more than a few steps, when suddenly he froze. A monstrous, clawed figure was pacing its way towards him from the kitchen. **"A PANTHER!"** Ian shrieked with all his might.

Max leaned over to see what was happening, as Ian fled at top speed. Without even looking where he was going, Ian dashed up the stairs and locked himself in the attic, leaving his little brother all alone. At the other end of the corridor was Marrameu, now a beast with large fangs and sharp claws. **IMPOSSIBLE!**

The fierce feline looked at the tiny human and charged towards him. Was that the end of Max?

No! The cat just wanted to be stroked. Ian heaved a big sigh of relief. Marrameu was still the same cuddly cat he'd known all his life. Although it wasn't a bad thing to have a panther as a pet, it was a lot to take on board.

As hard as it was to believe, Max now did not have a single doubt that his wish had come true! Somehow it had happened, but there was no time for scientific explanations. How many lies had Ian told him? What would happen next?

"Oh no! The pirate in the attic!" Max exclaimed.

Max raced up the stairs but when he managed to open the door, what he saw did not look like danger, quite the opposite. His brother was standing next to some treasure! Max drew closer to investigate. It was an old wooden chest, filled with gold coins and medallions. There was so much treasure it shone! Ian was so mesmerised, he'd forgotten about the panther.

"Now I can buy the new Playtrolendo X!" Ian said, his eyes lighting up.

"Ian, don't you understand? What if the pirate ghost appears?"

"Pirate? Are you serious? Can't you see? We're rich!"

"Yes, but listen," Max tried to explain.

Ian didn't listen and filled his pockets to the brim with treasure. However, before long there was a sinister sound of footsteps, scraping across the floor. Through gloom of the darkness, they could make out a skeleton with a peg leg, a hook for a hand, an eye patch and a skull wearing a large hat. It was the attic pirate! The two children trembled.

"Who dares touch my treasure?" she shouted in a thunderous voice.

She drew her pirate sword and pointed it at Max but then thought again and pointed it at Ian.

"**YOU!** Have you laid your dirty hands on my treasure?"

"Me? No. No way," he whimpered.

But just as Ian spoke those last words... **CRAAAACK!** Ian's pockets ripped open and a stream of coins fell to the ground. *Clink *clink *clink *clink. The pirate snorted, and Ian tried hard to keep smiling.

The boy tried to bluff his way out. "About that, before I'm falsely accused, if I may say one thin run Max! **RUN FOR YOUR LIFE!**" Ian picked up as many coins as he could from the ground and started running.

Max and the pirate were stunned. "Is he always like that?" she asked.

"Seems like it" Max replied, sadly.

"Shall I teach him a lesson?" she suggested.

"Yes, he deserves it."

And the bony pirate took off like a whirlwind after the lying boy. Max stood still for a moment but then reacted and ran as fast as he could to catch up with them. He hurried down the stairs and found his brother in the corner of the kitchen. He was curled up in a ball with his T-shirt pulled over his head. Marrameu panther and the pirate were scaring him with roars and swishing swords. They were turning everything upside down! Max walked over to see how his brother was doing and help fix things.

"Max, please, what's going on?" Ian said sticking his head out of his T-shirt like a turtle.

"Be quiet!" The pirate snapped.

"A-alright," he said as he hid again.

"As you can see," she continued, "others believed your scary lies. Now, if you want to go back, you will have to use the wishing rock and the three tries."

"Why are you speaking in rhyme?"

"Ian, listen to her!" said Max.

The pirate cleared her throat and continued with her lesson.

"You'll never lie again! That is going to be your wish. Understood?"

"Ok, I'll throw a stone and

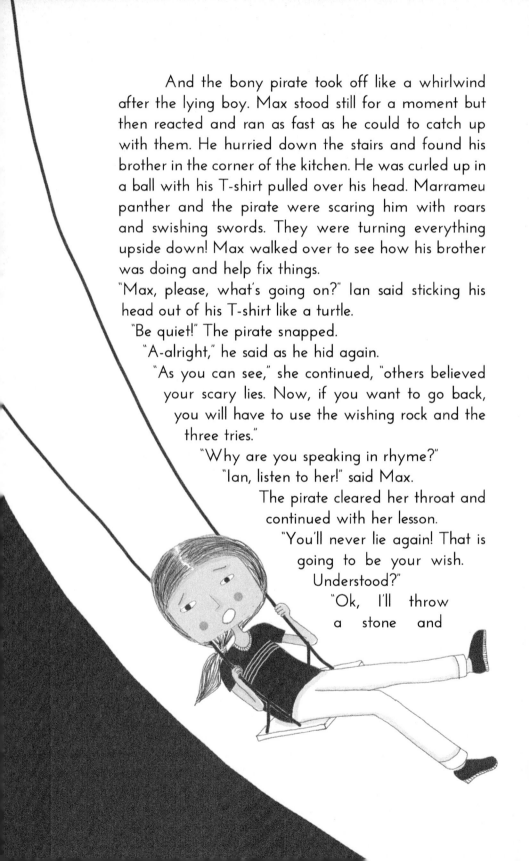

make a wish. Yes, I remember. Understood."

But Ian paid no attention and ran out screaming **"RUN FOR YOUR LIFE, MAX!"** He ran out into the garden, but as he was moving like a headless chicken, he tripped and fell over onto the swing, and started doing full circles like a washing machine.

"Help! Help!" he cried.

No matter what he did, he couldn't stop circling round and round, just like in his lie. A few minutes later the pirate, Marrameu panther and Max arrived, and stood staring at him.

"What was it? A hundred full circles?" Max laughed.

"Don't tease me," he cried out, "can't you see I need help?"

"So, you'll do it? You'll make a wish to stop telling lies?"

"Yes, yes, whatever you want! You throw the stone and I'll make the wish."

Max knelt down and picked up the first three stones he saw.

"At the count of three, ok?" One, two and Three," said Max.

"I wish I'd stop telling lies!" Ian yelled.

Max threw the first pebble. It bounced off his brother's backside, and then shot right into the pirate's eye.

"*Whoops," Max swallowed.

"I'm going to throw up," shouted Ian after 45 circles around on the swing.

Max readied himself then tried again...

"One, two and **THREE!**"

"I wish I'd stop telling lies!"

The pebble bounced off Ian's knee, shot up into the sky, and as if by magic, touched the wishing rock. Suddenly the swing stopped moving and Ian landed on the ground in a cloud of dust.

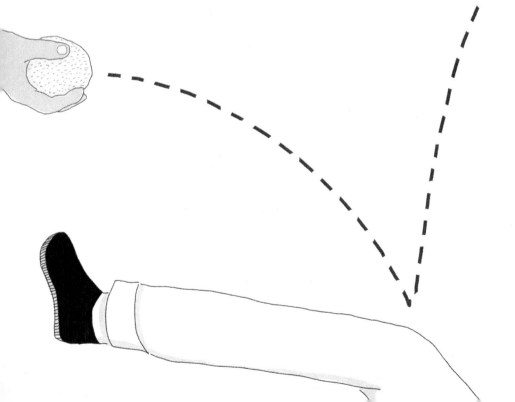

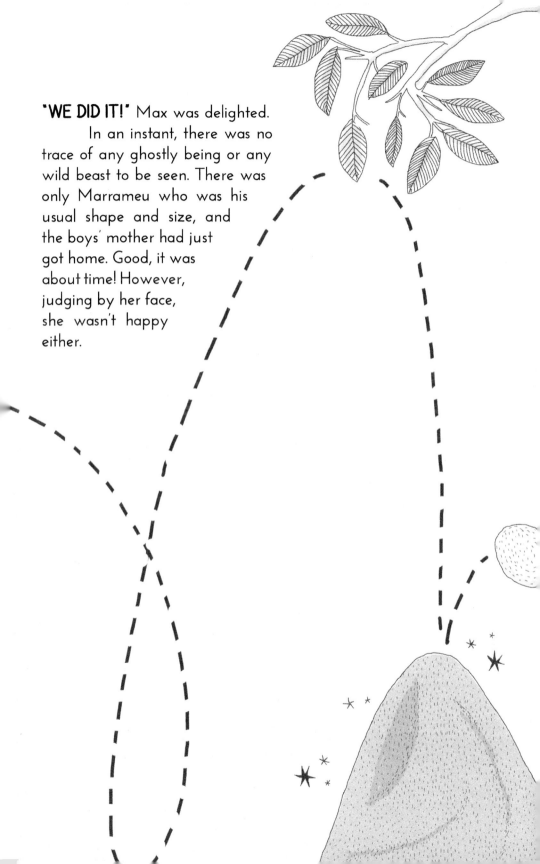

"WE DID IT!" Max was delighted.
In an instant, there was no
trace of any ghostly being or any
wild beast to be seen. There was
only Marrameu who was his
usual shape and size, and
the boys' mother had just
got home. Good, it was
about time! However,
judging by her face,
she wasn't happy
either.

"What happened in the kitchen?" she asked in disbelief. "Do we have a tiger at home now?!"

"Well, almost..." Max said with a half-smile.

"Max, was it you?"

"It was my fault," Ian confessed. "Mum, we need to talk."

Would Ian tell the truth for the first time? Since that would be an adult conversation, Max went into the house to do something else. He reflected on what had happened and understood that perhaps he believe everything that he was told too easily. And when you believe everything you're told, people take advantage of you. From now on he would listen more carefully!

Max was wandering through the house, distracted, when he noticed a box on the front table that looked familiar. The box was open and he was intrigued. He went to see what was in it - surely he wasn't doing anything wrong. Inside was a scroll that read: The Great Secret Map of the Universe. But before he could take a better look, his mother showed up and snatched it from his hands.

"Work stuff, you know."

Max was cross. What was that supposed to mean? However, the best thing was, after that very long and scary day, his mother changed her work hours so she could be home with them every afternoon. No one knows exactly what was said between his mum and Ian but, by being honest for the first time with his mother, Ian made his greatest wish come true.

And that's how the house stopped being haunted.

THE FIRST FLOWER OF SPRING

A story to turn the way we relate
to nature upside down

Along, long time ago... well no, not really that long ago, it could have happened only last week. Anyway, the story begins in a valley in the middle of the mountains. Hidden away there was a small town so beautiful that it felt like a fairy- tale town.

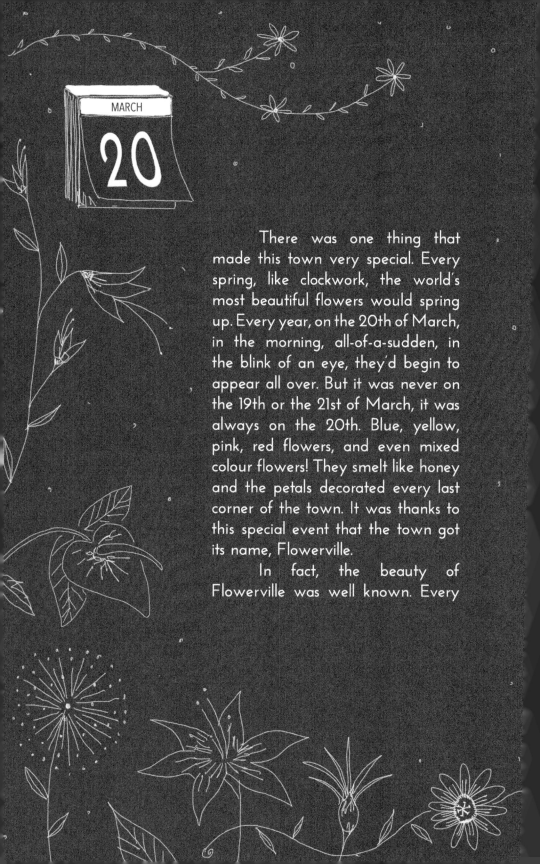

There was one thing that made this town very special. Every spring, like clockwork, the world's most beautiful flowers would spring up. Every year, on the 20th of March, in the morning, all-of-a-sudden, in the blink of an eye, they'd begin to appear all over. But it was never on the 19th or the 21st of March, it was always on the 20th. Blue, yellow, pink, red flowers, and even mixed colour flowers! They smelt like honey and the petals decorated every last corner of the town. It was thanks to this special event that the town got its name, Flowerville.

In fact, the beauty of Flowerville was well known. Every

spring, people would come from near and far to buy a bouquet, or simply take a picture and have lunch at the restaurant. On those days the town was so crowded that queues of tourists would gather in even the narrowest lanes. Some locals liked all the hustle and bustle and others less so.

Whether or not they enjoyed all the activity, the start of the new season was an important date on the Flowerville calendar. Early in the morning, the townspeople would all meet around the large flowerpot in the main square to see the first flower of spring. The day was even a holiday from school!

Like anywhere else, there were children in Flowerville, but there were two in particular - a brother and sister - who were little rascals. Their names were Lili and Dylan. How would one describe these little mischief-makers?

Lili

you could say she was hyperactive but lazy. That meant that she had the energy of a hurricane for some things and that of a log for others. Getting out of bed for school? She was a log. Getting up early to go to the spring festival? A hurricane!

Dylan,

on the other hand, was very different. A quiet and observant child. He could spend a whole day in silence and at night give a long explanation about the life of beetles. A child who, without a doubt, never stopped questioning everything.

As usual, Lili and Dylan were the first to set foot in the Plaza Mayor. Maybe it was too early, as there wasn't a single coloured petal to be seen yet. But they didn't mind. They knew that if they weren't the first to arrive, they wouldn't be able to see anything.

Little by little all the local residents turned up and sat down to wait for the first flower of spring. A few minutes went by, and then a few more minutes, and the minutes turned into hours. People began chatting anxiously amongst themselves.

WHAT TIME IS IT?

WHERE ARE THE FLOWERS?

WHAT'S THE MATTER?

The crowd grew more and more impatient and, to appease them, the Mayor made an appearance. He was a greying gentleman who liked to wear a very old-fashioned top hat. He turned on a megaphone and addressed the crowd.

DEAR CITY RESIDENTS, DON'T FRET!

WHY DON'T YOU GO BACK TO WORK

BEFORE THE TOURISTS GET HERE.

THE FIRST FLOWER WILL BLOOM ANY TIME

NOW AND WE MUST BE PREPARED.

EVERYTHING WILL BE FINE!

And everyone went back to their shops, restaurants and workshops. Only Lili and Dylan were left standing there. Dylan scratched his chin, slightly confused.
"Something doesn't make sense," he thought, "Everyone knows that in this town spring is as punctual as clockwork."
"Who knows?" replied his sister. "Maybe this year the flowers got tired of us."
"Don't be silly. That's not the way it works, I read it in a book."
"You know who has a lot of books? Moira!"
"Moira?" Dylan hesitated.
Moira was a retired schoolteacher who also happened to be an internationally renowned scholar of everything flower-related. Dylan suggested they go visit her, as he was sure that she was one of the few adults who would listen to them.

So they took the uphill road to get to Moira's home-laboratory. It wasn't too far, a ten-minute walk or so up the hill but it was so hot that they were both sweating like pigs.

"Ugh... I'm stopping here, I can't go on," Lili grumbled.

"I told you! This isn't normal, it's the 20th of March but it feels like the 20th of August!"

Lili, exhausted, sat down on a rock to rest. But, a second later she was back up on her feet and running into the forest like a whirlwind.

"Look, Dylan, look! **A ROSE!**" she shouted excitedly.

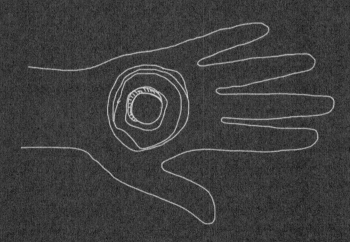

"It isn't a rose, Lili. It's a crushed plastic bottle!"

"Oh well, almost," his sister insisted.

The boy put the bottle in his backpack to throw in the yellow recycling bin later. However, suddenly they realised that wasn't the only thing that had been dumped there. The place was full of litter!

"That's dreadful!" Dylan exclaimed loudly.

Unfortunately, their backpack was too small, and there was no point in them trying to pick it up all up on their own. So, feeling a bit sad, they continued up to the top of the hill, where the flower expert lived.

They rang the doorbell and no one answered. They tried again and after a few minutes, the door creaked open. It was Moira, wearing her huge scientist glasses, which made tiny things look large.

'WELL, WELL,' she said, 'IF IT ISN'T LITTLE LILI, HOW YOU'VE GROWN! AND LOOK, YOUR BROTHER. JUST THE OTHER DAY HE WAS A BABY AND NOW, MY WORD, YOU'RE ENORMOUS!

"Excuse me," Lili interrupted.
The scientist took her special magnifying glasses off and realised that they weren't actually as tall as she had first thought. She laughed at her own mistake and invited them in. As soon as they came inside, the children were mesmerised by all her weird and wonderful apparatus. In fact, it was all so fascinating the children forgot for a moment why they were there.

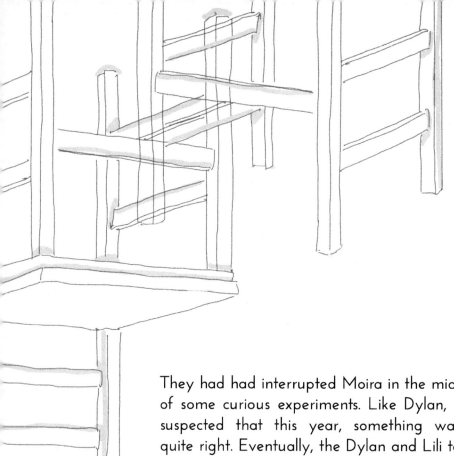

They had had interrupted Moira in the middle of some curious experiments. Like Dylan, she suspected that this year, something wasn't quite right. Eventually, the Dylan and Lili took a deep breath, and began bombarding her with questions.

"Have we gone from winter to summer?" Dylan began.

"It's so hot I broke out in a sweat getting here," Lili complained.

"And there isn't a flower in the whole valley! Only litter, everywhere."

"Children, I'm afraid this year the seasons are all over the place. The cars, the litter in the forest, the new factories... It's as if the flowers have got tired of us!" Moira concluded.

"I told you," said Lili to her brother.

"Impossible!" Dylan replied. "I read in a book that it takes years for these things to happen."

"Flowerville is a unique place," the teacher added. "It's very sensitive to changes."

Dylan was wide-eyed. There was no doubt about it, Moira's rigorous studies proved it! The problem was, there was no magic solution and, for now, there was only one thing they could do: **ALLOW NATURE TO TAKE A WELL-DESERVED REST.** They had to warn the Mayor, and everyone else, before it was too late! With no time to lose, Moira challenged the others to a race, to see who could reach the square first.

Lili won but, as she was four years older than her brother, it wasn't surprising. In any case, there was no one left in the square. Just a little girl who wouldn't take her eyes off the flowerpot.

"Hi," Dylan introduced himself.

But the girl didn't say a word – she was very focused on what she was doing.

"Do you know where all the adults have gone?" the boy continued.

It seemed that the cat had got her tongue. Lili waved her hand across the girls' face to see if she was sleeping with her eyes open, but the girl pushed her arm away.

"Can't you see I'm busy?"

And the girl continued to stare at that empty pot.

"Busy? Doing what?" Lili hesitated.

"I'm waiting for the first flower of spring to sprout. I'm a person with responsibilities. The Mayor personally asked me to do this!"

"The Mayor? Where is he now?" asked Dylan. It was important to find him!

"Don't you know? Everyone is in the town hall. They have called an emergency meeting!"

As there was no time to lose, the children ran as fast as their legs could carry them.

"DEAR RESIDENTS! I KNOW I SAID EARLIER THAT EVERYTHING WOULD BE FINE BUT THAT MAY NOT BE ENTIRELY TRUE... THIS MORNING WE ARE FACING THE WORST CRISIS IN THE HISTORY OF OUR TOWN. IT'S 11 A.M. NOW, AND NOT A SINGLE FLOWER HAS APPEARED. AND WITHOUT FLOWERS, THERE ARE NO TOURIST AND, WITHOUT TOURISTS, NO MONEY...

The man nearly fainted as he uttered these words, but he pulled himself together to continue his speech.

"THEREFORE, I AM OFFERING A LARGE REWARD TO ANYONE WHO CAN KEEP THE TOWN FROM LOSING MONEY!"

A hum of chatter filled the hall. Everyone wanted the reward but nobody dared to speak. Finally, a young bearded man in a palm tree print shirt raised his hand..

"I have an idea!" said the bearded man.

Unexpectedly, he took some very odd-looking glasses from his pocket and put them on.

"Virtual reality glasses! We'll hand them out and make everyone believe that the valley is, as always, full of flowers."

"I like your energy, young man. Can you come up to the stage and tell us more?" the mayor proposed.

The young man got up but, with the glasses on, he couldn't see the real world and fell flat on his face.

"An applause for the young man. Does anyone else have any ideas?" The mayor was getting impatient.

"I have one," said a mysterious businesswoman carrying a pile of folders.

She got up and went over to the microphone to explain her proposal to everyone. She opened up her folders and displayed a large poster that read: Flowerville 360° In a higher resolution than actual nature!

"I love it, I love it!" The Mayor applauded enthusiastically.

"If you can provide us with the money, our company can set up panoramic screens with images of flowers all over the valley this very afternoon. That way no one will notice anything."

"Consider it done!" said the Mayor.

'STOP!' yelled a little voice.

It was Lili and Dylan! The brother and sister rushed to the stage to get everyone's attention.

FLOWERVILLE 360°

"Don't you realise this is madness!" Dylan shouted loudly. "If you put up those screens, the real trees won't get any light and you'll make it even worse!"

"Trees take up a lot of space and need a lot of water. Putting up screens is much more environmentally-friendly," argued the mayor. "Right, children off you go now."

"Listen!" Lili insisted, wanting to give her input, "we have a real solution."

So she grabbed the microphone and told everyone about how the flowers had become tired of them. Yes, Flowerville was a very beautiful place, but also a very fragile one. If they wanted to keep it alive and full of colour, they would need to let it rest. The first step would be to explain this to the tourists and ask them to come back next year." By the end of her speech, the citizens of Flowerville didn't know whether or not to applaud. One coughed.

"Thanks for your contribution, little girl, but we want people to stay, not leave! Now go watch the flowerpot, we have work to do."

Nobody paid them any attention and the whole town went to work putting up the gigantic screens everywhere. In less than ten minutes the valley was filled with cranes. They were just horrid!

Lili and Dylan returned to the town square in the hope that a flower had sprung up and the madness would be over. The girl who was watching the flowerpot was still there and told them there was nothing new to report. Tired of watching, she left and handed the responsibility over to Lili and Dylan. But what could they do? Not only were they not going to let nature rest, they were going to put screens over it! Just then a couple appeared who were eager to buy a rose. But they couldn't find any shops open, so they walked up to the children, somewhat intrigued.

"Hi, this is Flowerville isn't it?" she asked.

"No, it's NoFlowerville," Lili replied sarcastically.

"Yes, it is," Dylan replied more politely, "but nature is closed for the holidays."

"Yeah, so bye." Lili finished the sentence by sticking her tongue out at them.

The couple left a little disappointed and empty-handed.

"One moment!" The girl had a brilliant idea. "I know where there's a flower!"

"Don't be silly!" Dylan replied, annoyed.

His sister opened his backpack and took out the plastic bottle that they had found in the forest. Maybe it didn't look exactly like a rose but, if she creased it here, folded it here and bent it there... with some little tricks that she'd seen online, Lilli created something amazing! She ran to catch up with the foreign couple to give them her creation and they happily accepted it. She then went back over to her brother rubbing her hands together, and smiling.

"Hehehe, they believed it."

Although it was a bit naughty, it gave Dylan a fantastic idea. To carry it out they needed Moira's help and everyone who was against the giant screens.

And so it was that lots of children from Flowerville, their parents and their former teacher, went to the forest to pick up as much plastic as they could. Some carried out the waste separation, while others made the recycled flowers.

They set up a stall next to the flowerpot in the square, where they gave away their creations to all the curious bystanders. There, Moira explained the big problem they had and how, for now, it was best to give Flowerville a break. So the visitors took home a beautiful recycled souvenir and they never forgot how important it was to take care of the environment. However, the visitors didn't stop there - when they discovered the Mayor's absurd plan, they went over to boo him.

"Boo! Out, out!" the visitors yelled.

"Boo!" the kids yelled.

"BOO!" Everyone yelled at once.

The Mayor didn't know what to do. What if they never voted for him again? The poor man had a panic attack and he decided to officially cancel his plan. The cranes and screens were removed forever! And, like the local residents, he too started recycling and making flowers (or at least whenever there was a photo opportunity).

"Your plan didn't turn out that badly in the end," Moira admitted to Lili and Dylan.

"Yes, but what about the first flower of spring?" Dylan asked innocently.

"Sadly, this story isn't over yet," the scientist concluded.

"You know what? I need a well-deserved rest," yawned Lili.

 After a long day full of adventure, they went to bed with the feeling that there was still a lot of work to be done. And although the spring flower wasn't to be seen again for a long time, from that day on, it became a tradition in Flowerville to give a recycled flower to celebrate the arrival of the spring.

JUNO AND THE MAGIC MARBLES

A story to turn upside down the limitations on
being able to be different

Do you remember when your birthday is? Course you do. Juno will never forget turning eight years old. And it was a unique day. Not only was she a year older, but it was also her first day at a new school! Would her schoolmates like her? When would she tell them that today was her birthday? Do people still do handstands? Anyone else would be a bit nervous, but Juno was different. She looked forward to everything and was always smiling.

Her dad, a struggling artist, didn't have much money and they had to move from a nice town to a big city in search of new opportunities. It was already the third time Juno and her dad had moved, as far as she could remember! But despite the fact that moving house was always a bother, her dad always found time to plan a surprise for his daughter. A very special one.

It was already 8.40 a.m. and there were only 20 minutes left until the school bell rang. Juno waited at the school gate with her father but she couldn't see the playground as it was surrounded by a metal fence.

What was all the shouting about? She imagined a giant playground to for clowning around in, full of playthings for having fun doing the things she liked doing. Meanwhile, her father took a small bag tied with a beautiful blue bow out of his pocket.

YEHHHHH   AHHHHHHH   GOAAAAAAL

"HAPPY BIRTHDAY" he said.

Juno's eyes opened wide. As it was her birthday and also her first day at school, she didn't expect anything until the afternoon (or later!). So this came as a surprise. She grasped the bag and undid the knot. What was inside it left her a little bewildered.

"Dice? What is it, a board game?" She asked curiously.

"No, no, they're marbles," said her father.

"Marbles? But marbles are round!"

"I haven't told you everything yet," he said with an air of mystery. "They're square because they're different and magical."

"Magical?" She repeated, perplexed.

Juno scratched her head, trying to get her head around the idea. In her other school she used to play a lot with marbles. In fact, she was quite good, but she was not sure if she could win with these cubes.

"You'll make lots of friends with them, you'll see."

The girl looked at him a bit sceptically. Her father always came up with birthday surprises that were a bit different. They were never toys advertised on TV or anything like that. He made them with his artist tools. To be honest, her father always claimed that the things he made were magic, but actually they weren't. In spite of this, who doesn't like getting an early present?

"Thanks a lot, Dad," she said with a big smile.

"Come on, it's getting late."

And so Juno came into the playground with her square marbles ready to make lots of friends.

However, the playground wasn't as she had imagined it from the noises she'd heard from outside. No see-saws, no slides. There was a large grey concrete rectangle with stripes painted on it. And lots of children running all over the place, kicking a ball around.

Juno almost got hit on the head by a ball but luckily it just missed and bounced in front of her.

"You! Out the way!" ordered one of the boys who was playing with the ball.

Without really understanding what was going on, she crossed the whole playing field by dodging players and balls flying everywhere. She finally reached safety, next to a wall where there was a rubbish bin. She took a deep breath but her relief was short-lived. A boy and a girl, who appeared out of nowhere, burst onto the scene.

"Who dares invade our turf?" he threatened.

"Hi, my name's Juno," the birthday girl answered innocently.

"This brat doesn't know who we are," the other girl snapped.

"Well no, it's my first day at this school. Sorry."

"I'm Captain Sparkles!"

"And I'm Gummo!"

"And we're members of the Tickle Gang! The strongest in the playground!" They yelled in unison.

They finished the sentence in a heroic pose, flexing their muscles. Following this presentation, Juno clapped.

"Why are you clapping? We're supposed to be scary!" The Captain groaned.

"Sorry." Juno pretended her legs were shaking. "Oooh! Is that better?"

"I recommend you **DO NOT** laugh at Captain Sparkles. She's eight and a half years old and she's really good at playing marbles!"

"Marbles?" **GREAT!** Look what I have!"

So Juno happily showed them the big surprise from her dad. The Tickle gang were speechless, then burst out laughing.

"This girl is nuts. These aren't marbles!" the Captain sneered, making fun of her.

"Yes, they are," Juno replied.

"I don't know who gave you those, but they were pulling your leg," she continued.

"They're marbles and they're also magical!"

"I'm telling you they aren't magical."

"Yes they are."

"No, they aren't!"

"I challenge you to a game, and then you'll see."

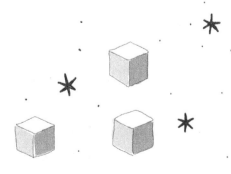

"You don't know who you're messing with," the boy teased. "Captain Sparkles has won all 300 marble matches! Against me, of course," tailing off quickly.
"Let's make a deal. If I lose, you'll never see me around here again."
"Done." The Captain agreed with a handshake.

They sat down and drew a circle on the ground to play, and something incredible happened!
"She beat you, she beat you!" Gummo couldn't believe it.
"Tickle Gang emergency meeting!" the Captain announced.
They huddled round so no one would hear them.
"Captain, Captain, she beat you!" Do you think they really are magical?

"Could be. It's the only explanation - I never lose," she said with wounded pride. "What should we do? Will you resign as Captain?"

"**NEVER!** We can only do one thing."

"Crush her?"

"**NO!** Accept her as an honorary member of the Tickle Gang!"

"Honorary? I'm not honorary," the boy complained.

"If she joins us, no one will know that she beat me. Understand?"

"So? Are they magical or not?" Juno stuck her head into the meeting.

"Mmm, yes, yes! Of course they are! In fact, we're so impressed that you can join our gang right now, as an honorary member!"

"Wow!" Juno thought, they must be magical, she had never made friends **THAT QUICKLY.**

"Come, I'll show you our Tickle Gang turf," Gummo said seriously.

He turned and pointed to the rubbish bin.

"From here to as far as the eye can see is ours!" Juno squinted her eyes to see better.

"Don't worry, I've drawn a map to guide us."

"Wow, I hope I don't get lost," Juno replied, a little embarrassed.

"Didn't you know? In this playground, you can only play with the ball," said the Captain.

"With the ball? Only?"

"Yes, it's what everyone does!"

"So why don't you do it?"

"It's weird, but we don't like it."

"I'm not very good at it," the boy revealed.

"And what does everyone else do?"

"Yeah, well, we do what we can on the edges, that's why it's so important to protect the gang's turf!"

To Juno it seemed quite unfair, but before she could tell them what she

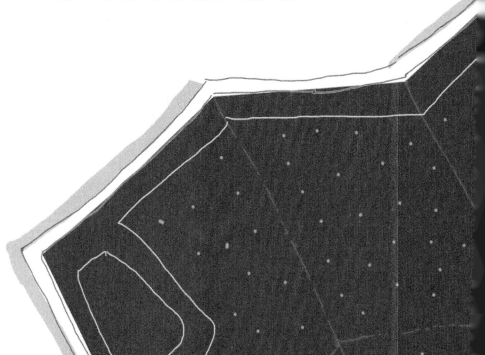

thought, the school bell rang to announce that classes were starting.

After a couple of hours or so, the bell rang again. This time it was announcing break time. The kids flooded outside to have fun. The kids with the ball instantly took over the entire playground, and the rest of the children hung out in the corners.

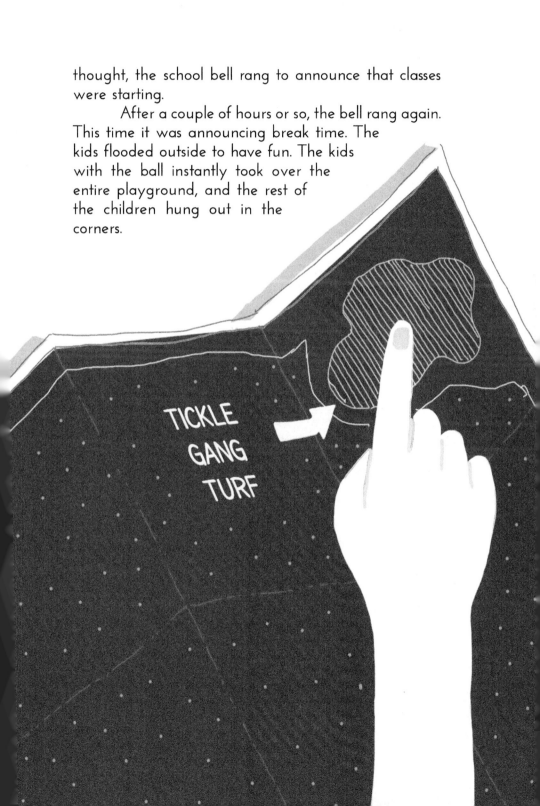

TICKLE
GANG
TURF

TAG, YOU'RE IT

The Tickle Gang rushed over to where the rubbish bin was so that they could have some space to play. But unfortunately, their territory was much smaller than it was earlier. The ball people had set up a new goal post with two backpacks. Now they couldn't even put their marbles on the ground!

"Oh well, it's happened again," Gummo complained, as he tore off a piece of his map.

"Why don't we tell the teacher?" Juno questioned.

"Oh right, and be a tell-tale on your first day? That is **NOT** our style!"

"Then we will stand up to them!" The new girl was excited.

"You're crazy! We'll just go somewhere else," Gummo replied.

So they walked around the edge of the cement field to see if they could find another place to put down their marbles. On one side they found two girls who were tapping each other's backs.

"They're playing tag, but since they have less than a metre to run around in, the games are very short," the captain explained.

TAG, YOU'RE IT

So they walked a few more steps towards the bushes.

"SHHHHHHHHHHHHHHHHH,"

Gummo whispered, "this is the hide-and-seek area...just
pretend you can't see them, that way they won't get angry."

They walked a little further until they reached a fountain. There were two children making mud cakes. "The best break-time cakes are made here but since another goalpost was set up in the sandbox, they only have one ingredient: water."

OH NO! IT'S
EVAPORATED
AGAIN!

ANOTHER
ORDER
CANCELLED.

After going all the way round, they couldn't find even an inch of space to play marbles. So they returned to their small turf, which was even more microscopic than the last time they were there. Someone had set up another goal! I mean, how many did they need?

WHAT SHALL WE PLAY?

By the end of school day, which seemed endless if you didn't like school, finally the bell rang that meant "enough learning for today!" The children stormed out. And, once again, the ball children returned to hog the whole playground. Even after classes were over, they were still there! How could that be?

"Are you crazy? The ball people rule the playground. No-one can ever question them!" The captain reminded her.

"I don't care; I've got my magic marbles."

"They're not magic!"

"Yes they are, you even said so yourself earlier."

"I didn't want to admit that you'd beaten me," she confessed.

Juno was undeterred by her words, and headed out into the middle of the field with her square marbles. "People with the ball, listen up!" she shouted at the top of her lungs.

But no one paid the slightest attention to her. Everyone carried on just the same, running around kicking the ball. And seeing this, Juno had an idea: to pick up the ball in her hands! That was forbidden in the ball kicking game. "Handball!" some screamed, "Penalty!" cried another, "No, she's offside!" they yelled from further away. The general confusion brought the game to a halt.

"Great, now listen up!" Juno began.

"Hey you, give it back to us!" One boy wearing a striped shirt threatened her.

"No! The rest of us need space too!"

"Don't be a baby. Playing ball is what everyone does. They talk about it all day, at all hours, everywhere. If you want to be successful in life you have to play ball. And anyone who doesn't want to go anywhere can get out of our way."

"We've had enough of being pushed around! It's not fair that we have to settle for a little corner. What we play is our way of being who we are. Without any space we can't be ourselves."

"   Don't bother me with your little speeches. Find somewhere else and put up a sign that says 'the cry baby corner'."

"Why should I make signs? The playground belongs to everyone!"

"Sure, give me my ball back now."

"I know! I'll give it back to you if you beat me at marbles."

"Marbles? Do people still play that?" he sneered mockingly.

"Are you afraid?

"Okay then, but since I don't have marbles I'll use the ball instead," he snapped back.

"I don't care," she said, "I'll use my marbles, which are magic."

"Juno, no!" Captain Sparkles warned her.

But she didn't listen and showed off her brand new square marbles. Everyone held their breath and no one dared to say anything.

"I feel sorry for you. Those are painted dice," the boy said laughing.

"They're marbles and they're magic. My dad gave them to me for my birthday."

"It's your birthday?" The captain was surprised.

"Yes! But I was a little embarrassed to say so," she confessed.

"Well, here's my birthday present, little girl" the boy interrupted, "your father lied to you."

"We'll see about that," she was sure of herself.

They put the ball and the cube in the centre of the circle and got ready for the match. The entire playground watched them expectantly. It was clearly a very one-sided game. The boy took his run-up and...

Juno was on the verge of crying, but she managed to hold back the tears.

Juno, wordless, went to pick up her dice, which had been shot across the courtyard. As she walked away, she felt sad, and thought that she would never find her place in this playground, since she was different from the others. But she suddenly stopped, and noticed how Captain Sparkles and Gummo hadn't moved an inch. They had no intention of leaving!

"I said off!" The boy was beginning to lose his temper.

Bit by bit, the whole school copied the Tickle Gang and stood there still like statues. The children playing tag, hide-and-seek and the pastry

chefs, all joined them.

"OFFFFFFFF!" the enraged boy repeated.

But no one paid any attention to his orders. In the end, even the ball players came to a halt and stood still! Juno's words had touched their hearts. It didn't matter whether her marbles were square or if she had won or lost, the playground belonged to everyone! This time Juno did cry, but with tears of happiness. **WHAT AN AMAZING BIRTHDAY SURPRISE!**

From that day on, break time was reaaally different. Some of the goal posts turned out to be swings and slides – brilliant! The Tickle Gang's turf was now so vast that Gummo needed half a page to draw his map. The children playing hide-and-seek discovered a thousand new hiding places and games of tag now lasted up to three days. Also, the pastry chefs were so successful that they opened a chain of

restaurants. Luckily, for Captain Sparkles, marbles were back in fashion and she proved that she was still one of the best. And as everyone now wanted them in different shapes, Juno's father had his work cut out for him for quite some time!

And Juno? Well, she played all those things and more! And, hard as it is to believe, one day she even tried playing football. She discovered she was actually pretty good, and signed up for the local team, where she scored lots of goals.

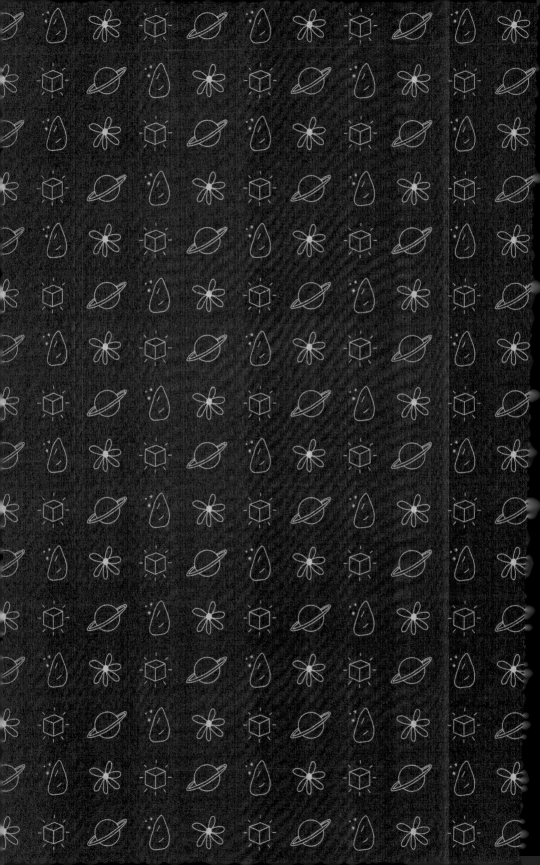

Printed in Great Britain
by Amazon

81582320R00066